Property of
BRIDGEPORT PUBLIC LIBRARY
North End Branch

by PHILIP PREECE
illustrated by BRADFORD KENDALL

Shade Books are published by Stone Arch Books
151 Good Counsel Drive, P.O. Box 669
Mankato, Minnesota 56002
www.stonearchbooks.com

Library of Congress Cataloging-in-Publication Data
Preece, Philip.
Carnival of horrors / by Philip Preece ; illustrated by Bradford Kendall.
p. cm. — (Nightmare Park)
"Shade Books"—T.p. verso.
Summary: When Ben tries to hide from bullies at a carnival, he is drawn into a sideshow that promises to make his dreams of popularity and good grades come true, if only he signs a contract agreeing to give up a few minutes of his time.
ISBN 978-1-4342-1615-1 (lib. bdg.)
[1. Supernatural—Fiction. 2. Carnivals—Fiction. 3. Bullies—Fiction. 4. Schools—Fiction. 5. Family life—Fiction.] I. Kendall, Bradford, ill. II. Title.
PZ7.P9118Car 2010
[Fic]—dc22

2009003783

Creative Director: Heather Kindseth
Graphic Designer: Hilary Wacholz

Printed in the United States of America

TABLE OF CONTENTS

CHAPTER 1

THE CHASE

It was dark, and Ben was running.

His breath came in painful gasps and his side hurt from the effort. As he burst out of the trees, he paused. He didn't know where to go next.

Ahead of him, across the empty fields, he could see the lights of the fair. It glowed like a fiery city, a blaze of color in the darkness. Music drifted toward him across the emptiness.

If he could get there, he'd be safe. But he could hear his pursuers crashing through the woods behind him.

Ben was no wimp, but there were three of them: Mark, Lee, and Danny. They were bullies who always picked on people who were alone.

Ben looked again at the dark empty fields stretching ahead of him. He wasn't sure if he could make it.

"Come on, he's here!"

The shout came from somewhere behind him. It sounded frighteningly close.

Like a shot, Ben took off running again.

Nobody usually went to the edge of the park. It was hard to run there, since the grass was so tall.

He could hear the hunters' heavy footsteps behind him. They weren't shouting anymore. They were silent, angry, saving their breath for running, determined to get their prey.

They were gaining on him.

Ben thought he could hear their tense breathing. He could almost feel it on the back of his neck.

He used all of his energy to pull ahead. He left them behind. He burst between the dark backs of two trailers. Then, finally, he was among the bright lights and noise of the fair.

He urgently pushed through the crowd. He had to get away, as far away from them as possible. He had to lose himself in the fair.

All around him, people were shouting and smiling, having a good time. Some of them held balloons and fluffy stuffed monkeys they'd won.

Groups of girls walked by with their arms linked together. Guys were pushing each other and laughing.

He was surrounded by people. But at the same time, Ben had never felt so alone. He was afraid.

What if his pursuers caught him? Would anybody try to stop them, even in this crowd?

He didn't think so. He turned and ran blindly on. He needed to put as much distance as possible between himself and his tormentors.

People were screaming with excitement as they whirled around on the rides. Bright, colored lights flashed on and off in time to the loud music that was blasting out.

Ben hurried through the fair. Everyone around him seemed to be having a good time.

There was no sign of anyone following him. He was sure no one would find him in the crowd.

Soon, he began to relax. He'd stay in the fair for a while, he decided, until he was sure he was safe. Then he'd make his way home.

At the edge of the fair, Ben saw a brightly lit tent. There was a crowd in front of it.

REAMLAND

Dreamland, the lights said. Tall gas jets flared on either side of a small stage.

A man in a black coat was calling out, "Come one, come all. Don't miss the chance of a lifetime. See your dreams come true. We have the very latest machinery. We can show your most secret thoughts."

Just then, a girl came out of a door at the back of the stage. She was smiling and excited. She waved to her waiting friends.

"I saw it!" she screamed. "My secret dream!" Her friends giggled. "It was amazing," the girl said.

Ben felt himself being pushed to the front of the crowd. Suddenly, he was being pressed against the stage. The man in black smiled and reached down a hand to lift him up.

"Come on," the man said. "You'll be safe up here."

Ben noticed movement out of the corner of his eye. Mark and the others had reached the back of the crowd where Ben had been standing just a minute ago.

He was trapped. Everyone could see him as he stood up there on the stage.

"Great!" the showman said loudly, smiling. He had a black mustache and dark, laughing eyes. "Here's a young man who wants to see his dreams come true. You're not afraid, are you?" he asked Ben, smiling widely.

As if from nowhere, a girl appeared. Ben thought she must be the showman's assistant. She was beautiful. She was wearing a bright red dress.

"Look after the gentleman, please, Lola," said the showman.

Lola smiled at them both. Then she took Ben's hand.

Ben allowed her to lead him across the stage. But instead of going through the door at the back, he found himself being led toward another door off to one side. He hadn't noticed the other door before. Suddenly, Ben felt nervous.

The showman walked up next to him.

"The main door's only for ordinary people," the showman whispered. "This one's special. It's for people who dare to take a chance. People who actually want to make their dreams come true."

Ben wasn't sure. He didn't want anyone to think he was a coward.

As he hesitated, he looked over his shoulder. Mark, Lee, and Danny were pushing their way forward through the crowd.

"A special door," repeated the showman, "for people like you. If you dare."

With a last nervous glance back at the bullies, Ben let himself be led through the doorway, into the blackness inside.

CHAPTER 2

VISIONS

At first he saw only darkness.

In the dark, Ben felt himself being guided to a cushioned chair. The showman's hand gripped his shoulder tightly.

Confused, Ben sat still for a moment. Then, suddenly, a row of TV screens turned on.

"Now!" said the showman.

On the screens, Ben saw himself hurrying across the fields just a few minutes ago. He was being followed by the bullies.

Ben watched in amazement as his face was shown in a huge close-up. He looked worried, frightened.

"Watch," said the showman.

Then Ben saw himself at school. He was in class, and the teacher was yelling at him.

Ben remembered that day. He'd gotten the worst grade in the class on the math test.

"There's no excuse," the teacher said. "You're lazy. Or you're stupid, getting these low grades." The class laughed.

Ben watched his own face. It looked as if he might cry.

He saw the faces of his classmates, one after another. Some of the boys were sneering. A girl was laughing at him.

This time Ben said nothing.

The pictures changed, and he saw himself at a school dance. He remembered that too. He was standing alone. Everyone else was having a good time.

He watched himself as he walked across and asked a girl to dance. He saw her expression before she turned away to giggle with her friends.

Ben squirmed with shame as he relived the moment. That was so stupid of him. After all, it was Lisa, the prettiest girl in the school. He'd never had a chance.

The lights came on slowly. The show seemed to be over.

Ben hoped no one could see his burning face. He'd just watched some of his worst nightmares — and they were all true.

Ben jumped up quickly. He couldn't wait to get out of there.

"Not a pretty sight, was it?" asked the showman.

Ben had to agree. He'd never realized before just how much of a joke he was. He sometimes felt like a fool, but he'd never guessed he looked as bad as that.

The showman went on, "Now we have something very special to show you. We have an incredible new process here at Dreamland. It really can make all your dreams come true!"

Lola, the assistant, came over. She smiled kindly at Ben.

She helped him back into his chair. Then she patted his arm gently.

The lights dimmed again. The screens showed the classroom.

This time, what happened was completely different. The teacher was reading the test results, and she was just coming to Ben's name.

But when she said his grade, Ben could hardly believe what she was saying. This time he had gotten the best grade in the class!

He saw the amazed expressions of his classmates, and heard the teacher telling him how smart he was.

The whole class applauded. The sound roared in Ben's ears, echoing louder and louder.

Then the action switched to another scene. Lisa, the girl he liked, the one who had laughed at him at the dance, was walking up to him.

She told him how great it was that he'd done so well on the test. She was smiling at him. Her friends were all smiling at him too.

Ben saw the expressions on the faces of the other boys. They were all jealous. For once, he was a success!

The scene changed and he recognized the schoolyard. The bullies were there.

Ben watched them head toward him in front of everyone. He winced, sure of what was going to happen. They'd beat him up and he'd be totally embarrassed. Everyone would laugh.

The next thing he knew, Mark was flat on his back with a surprised expression on his face. Everyone was laughing. The other two bullies ran off.

Ben blinked as the lights came up.

"That's how it could be, Ben," the showman said. "We can make your secret dreams come true."

"Really?" asked Ben.

He wanted it. He wanted to be what he'd seen on the screen. He didn't want to be the boy he really was.

"What do I have to do?" he asked.

The showman smiled. "It's easy," he said. "You don't have to do a thing."

Then Ben had a moment of doubt. "Wait a second," he said. "What's the catch?"

"Absolutely no catch," said the man. "We're here to make people's dreams come true. There's just a small management charge. Nothing you can't afford."

"How much?" asked Ben doubtfully. He didn't have a job. He didn't even get an allowance.

The showman said, "The charge for making each dream come true? Oh, just a few minutes of your time."

That didn't seem like much. Ben frowned.

"Yes," the showman said. "Just a few short minutes of time. You've got your whole life in front of you. You'll never miss a minute here and there."

"Why do you want them?" Ben asked.

"Oh, let's just say we find them very useful," the showman said.

The screens turned on again. There, smiling, was one huge picture of Ben. He was happy, triumphant.

Ben thought about Lisa smiling back at him. He thought about his classmates clapping. "Okay," he said finally. "What do I have to do?"

"Just sign here," the showman said.

Lola held a huge book open in front of Ben. She handed him a strange pen. It was like a long feather with a sharp point.

"Careful," said the showman, "it's sharp. Oh, too late."

Ben felt a terrible pain. "Ow!" he shouted. He'd cut his finger on the point.

"Never mind," the showman said. "Just sign here and it'll all be over in a moment."

He pointed to a dotted line at the bottom of the page. The book was made of some stiff, thick paper and covered in strange, old-fashioned writing.

Ben signed his name carefully on the line. He was startled to see that the ink was as red as blood. "There," he said.

The showman slapped the book shut with a snap. "Thank you," he said.

"Is that it?" asked Ben.

"Oh yes, that's it," the showman said. He laughed, showing long white teeth. For a moment he reminded Ben of a wolf.

Ben felt himself being helped out of his seat and pushed toward the door.

The showman's sharp fingers gripped his shoulder. It was almost painful.

As he saw the lights of the fair again, Ben suddenly felt nervous. The showman's hand had felt just like a claw.

CHAPTER 3

AN ACCIDENT

The next day Ben went to school as normal. The night before seemed like a dream. He wasn't sure whether it had been a good dream or not.

He'd forgotten all about it by the last class of the day. There'd been a test in math the day before. The teacher was reading the test results.

Ben wasn't really paying attention. He knew he hadn't studied hard enough.

He was shocked when his teacher read his grade. Just like in the vision at Dreamland, he had actually gotten the best grade!

Everything seemed to spin around him. People were turning around and smiling at him.

The teacher congratulated him, just like he'd seen on the TV screens. Then the whole class started clapping.

After school, Ben couldn't wait to get home. A couple of his classmates slapped him on the back on the way out of school. "Great job," they said. "You were amazing."

Ben ran home as fast as he could. He burst into the house, shouting. "Mom!" he yelled. "Guess what!"

His mother came out of the kitchen.

"Guess what!" he said again. "I got the best grade in the class on my math test!"

Mom didn't say anything.

"Everyone was clapping," he said. "It was great!"

She still didn't say anything. He looked at her more closely. Her eyes were red. It looked as if she'd been crying.

"What's the matter?" he asked.

"It's Jip," Mom said.

Jip was Ben's dog. Ben had owned him since he was a puppy.

"There was an accident," Mom went on. "He was hit by a car. I don't know how he got out to the road. I was sure I'd closed the front door, but somehow — I'm so sorry, honey."

Ben's good mood disappeared. He was hardly listening to what his mother had to say. The dog was at the vet's. Ben felt terrible.

"Is he going to be all right?" he asked quietly.

"They aren't sure," Mom said sadly. She put a hand on his arm. "The vet thinks we should be ready for the worst. They'll let us know soon what they think will happen to Jip."

Ben was silent. A minute ago, he'd been on top of the world. But a lot can happen in a minute.

Ben felt depressed for the rest of the evening.

* * *

The next day at lunchtime, as Ben went out to the schoolyard, he saw a sight he'd been dreading. The three bullies were coming toward him.

Mark got right in his face. "You thought you got away with it the other night, didn't you?" Mark said. "Well, your luck just ran out, kid!"

He poked Ben hard in the chest. Mark's other hand was already clenched into a hard fist.

Lee and Danny laughed. Everyone was watching.

Ben wasn't sure exactly what happened, but the next thing he knew, Mark was lying flat on his back gasping for breath. He looked really surprised. Everybody burst out laughing.

Lee and Danny looked shocked. Mark was the toughest kid in the whole school. No one had ever messed with him before. Lee and Danny ran off. Mark jumped to his feet and sped off after them.

Everybody crowded around Ben, congratulating him. It was great. He was a hero, even if he hadn't actually done anything.

It felt good to be popular. Really good.

On the way home, Ben remembered Jip. He hoped his dog was going to be all right.

Dad and Mom were in the living room when Ben got home. Dad didn't usually come home until late.

They sat there silently. Dad looked upset. Ben felt his heart pound in his chest.

"We have some bad news," said Mom.

"Is it Jip?" Ben asked.

"No," Mom said. "He's still at the vet. There's been no change. It's your dad. He lost his job."

It was quiet in the house that night. Everyone was depressed.

Ben had a lot to think about. He went to bed early that night, but he lay awake for hours. He couldn't fall asleep. He couldn't stop worrying about the bargain he had made at Dreamland.

A few minutes of time hadn't seemed like a high price to pay for having his dreams come true. But a lot could happen in a minute. Now it seemed that for every good thing, something bad happened.

Getting things you hadn't worked for was cheating. He could see that now. He hated to think what might happen next.

* * *

He was just leaving school the next day when a girl came up to him.

It was Lisa, the prettiest girl in the school, the one he liked.

"Hello," Lisa said.

Ben had wanted to go out with Lisa ever since he'd first seen her. He had been so embarrassed when she'd turned him down at the dance.

"I loved the way you stood up to those bullies," she said. "They've been getting away with it for too long. It was really cool, what you did yesterday."

Ben couldn't believe it. She was looking at him as if she really liked him.

Ben felt a chill running down his spine. It was all happening just like he'd seen on the screens at Dreamland.

He turned away, suddenly scared of what might happen next. This time he was really afraid to go home.

CHAPTER 4

RUN DOWN

When Ben got home, his mother wasn't there. His dad was.

"Where's Mom?" he asked.

"She had to go to the hospital," Dad said.

Ben felt as if a bony hand was slowly squeezing his heart.

"It's your grandma. She's very sick," Dad explained.

Ben felt his stomach turn over. He knew that something was very wrong, and he was pretty sure it had something to do with Dreamland. The dream was turning out to be a nightmare.

When is this going to end? he wondered.

He tried to shut out the thoughts that were coming to him. Ever since he'd signed the book, his dreams had come true, just like he'd been promised. But then terrible things had happened too: the dog, his dad's job, and now Grandma.

He could have gotten the best grade in the class by studying. He could have really stood up to the bullies. It hadn't been that hard. And maybe Lisa really liked him. Perhaps it was easier to be a success than he had thought it was.

But now he was afraid of what might happen next. He didn't want any more good luck. He wished he could go back and start all over again.

He had to go back to the fair, back to Dreamland. Somehow he had to cancel the contract. Otherwise, who knew what price he'd have to pay for his next piece of good luck.

After dinner, Dad said they should go to the hospital. Ben couldn't stop thinking about the deal he'd made.

He felt terrible about Grandma being sick. It was all his fault. If he hadn't gone to Dreamland in the first place, Grandma wouldn't be sick.

Ben had to stop what was happening. Right away.

He had to see the showman and explain. If Ben could talk him into canceling the contract, then all these terrible things would stop.

"I can't go to the hospital," Ben told his dad. "I have too much homework."

Dad frowned. "But your grandma's sick," he said. "This is serious. And your mom will want to see you. Leave the homework for later. It can't be that important."

"It is," said Ben. "I have to hand it in tomorrow. I'll be in trouble if I don't. It was due last week."

Dad was starting to look annoyed. "Your mother's going to be upset," he said. "But I don't have time to stand around talking about it. I have to go make sure they're all right."

He frowned again, as if he knew Ben was up to something. But then he left, and Ben was alone.

Ben breathed a deep sigh of relief. His dad was always telling him what to do. None of his friends' parents treated them like that.

It made Ben really angry sometimes, the way his parents treated him like he was a little kid. It wasn't fair.

He didn't have time to worry about that now. He had to get to the fair and put his plan in motion. Then everything would be all right.

As soon as he heard his dad's car pulling out of the driveway, Ben grabbed his coat. Then he quickly headed out the door. He didn't have much time.

It was dark outside. Ben started running. The sooner he got to the fair, the sooner he'd be back.

If he wasn't back by the time Mom and Dad got home, he would be in even more trouble. He just hoped that he could talk to the showman, make him see that Ben just needed to get out of the contract.

Then all the trouble would be fixed. Jip would be all right, Grandma wouldn't be sick, and Dad would get another job.

Ben ran toward the fair.

The fair was crowded, as usual. People were screaming as they whirled around on the rides, but to Ben, they didn't sound as if they were enjoying themselves.

It sounded like they were scared to death.

He searched the fair anxiously, looking for Dreamland. It was taking forever. For some reason, Ben couldn't remember how to get there.

When he finally found it, he could see that something was terribly wrong. There were no lights on the stage. Dreamland didn't seem to be open.

When Ben neared the stage, it seemed to him that Dreamland hadn't been open in a very long time. Maybe years.

Ben frowned. He looked closer. The paint was peeling, light bulbs in the Dreamland sign were missing, and some of the steps had rotted away completely. The main entrance was all boarded up.

How could it have gotten so run down in such a short time?

EAM AND

It was quiet at the edge of the fair. Ben suddenly felt cold.

He turned, looking for someone to help him. There was a small food stand nearby. The man running it was just closing up.

"Excuse me," said Ben. "What happened to Dreamland?"

The man looked at him as if he was crazy. Then he shrugged and turned away.

Ben felt a shiver of fear. How was he going to end the contract now?

He had to see the man in black. If he didn't, there was only one way left. It was a long shot, but Ben had no choice. He had to get his hands on that contract. He would come back later when no one was around. He was going to have to break in.

All the lights were on in the house when he got back. Ben's heart sank. He must have been at the fair longer than he'd thought. As he opened the door, he could hear Dad's voice. He sounded really angry.

"And he's lying to us now," Dad said. "That's what makes it worse."

Ben walked into the living room. Dad turned around.

"Where do you think you've been?" Dad shouted. He didn't wait for an answer. "We've been worried sick. I thought you had some homework to do."

Ben looked at Mom. She was sitting at the table with her head in her hands.

"Where have you been?" shouted his dad again.

Ben took a deep breath. "I went to the fair," he began, but before he could explain his dad interrupted.

"The fair?" Dad yelled. "You've been to the fair? Out enjoying yourself with your grandma in the hospital? I can't believe you. You don't care about anybody but yourself!"

That wasn't true. Ben did care about everyone else. But how could he explain?

Ben opened his mouth to speak, but no words came out. He wanted to tell them that he'd been trying to help everybody, trying to stop everything from going wrong. But how could he tell them about Dreamland and the bargain that he'd made?

"That's it," Dad said. "You're grounded."

Ben's mouth dropped open. He couldn't be grounded.

He had to get back to the fair. He had to make everything all right again. He had to see the showman.

But what could he say? How could he tell them he was trying to save them from the terrible things that had happened, and maybe even worse things to come?

For the first time since Ben got home, his mother raised her head. She looked straight at him.

The look on her face made Ben's stomach hurt. He wished he could make them understand. Sadly, Ben turned and left the room.

There was only one thing to do. He'd have to wait until everyone was asleep.

Then he would leave. He'd make one final attempt to get back into Dreamland.

He had one last chance before it was too late.

CHAPTER 5

THE SHOWMAN

Ben lay silently in the dark. He waited until his parents were in bed and everything was quiet. Then as quietly as he could, he found a hammer and left the house. The fields were empty. He could see the shadowy shape of the fair in the darkness.

When he reached the fair, all the rides were closed. The whole place was empty. He felt as if he was being watched from the empty food stands and darkened rides.

At last, he reached Dreamland. His footsteps sounded loud as he walked up the rotting steps. He used his hammer to pry the boards away from the door. They resisted at first, but soon they gave way. The boards made a terrible cracking noise that sounded as loud as an explosion in the night.

It was pitch black inside. Ben stepped forward uncertainly. Suddenly, a flame sprang up in front of him. Then another, and another, until a ring of flames surrounded Ben.

A laugh came out of the shadows. It was the man in black.

"Ah, Ben," the showman said. "So you have found us. Welcome. What can we do for you?"

"I want my contract back," Ben said nervously.

"But Ben, we made a bargain," the showman said.

"I know," Ben said. "But I want my contract back anyway."

"Didn't you get what you were promised?" the showman asked.

"Yes," Ben said. He wanted to say it hadn't been fair, that he hadn't understood what he was agreeing to. But somehow he just couldn't find the right words.

"You signed, Ben," the showman said. "Look."

As the man spoke, the light got brighter. There was a wide, round pit in the middle of the room.

Smoke was rising out of the pit, lit by a fiery glow from underneath. A steep flight of stairs went straight down into the pit's depths.

As Ben watched, Lola came slowly up the stairs, wrapped in coils of smoke. She was smiling, holding the book that Ben's contract was in.

Lola's crimson dress looked as if it were on fire. She handed the book to the showman and went back down the stairs.

The showman opened the book. He flipped through the huge pages. Ben could see that there were dozens of contracts just like his.

"Where is it?" the showman mumbled. "Ah, yes, here."

He held the book open for Ben to see. "There you are. That is your signature, isn't it?" the showman asked.

"Yes," Ben admitted.

The showman started to close the book.

Ben knew what he had to do. With a desperate lunge, he reached for the book. His fingers grabbed the edge of the parchment and held on. He had to get it. He had to rip out the page with his signature on it.

The showman pulled back. For a moment they teetered on the edge of the pit. Flames flared up from the depths below.

Ben held on to the page as hard as he could. He was being pulled nearer and nearer to the flames. Just then, he felt the page beginning to tear.

Ben gave one last, desperate tug. The page ripped straight across.

The showman hung for a moment over the edge of the hole. Then he fell backward into the pit. Flames shot up to the ceiling.

Ben looked down in horror. The showman was gone, taking the book and the contract with him. Now Ben would never be free.

The flames rose up above his head. Smoke swirled around him, filling the room. He took a step backward, trying to feel his way to the door.

Smoke and flames were everywhere. He was choking.

Then Ben felt himself falling, falling, falling . . .

CHAPTER 6

MORNING

Ben found himself wandering in a maze. Everything was dark. He thought he saw a light far ahead.

The light grew brighter. Ben walked toward it. He heard a voice speaking his name, over and over.

He opened his eyes.

He was lying on the cold damp ground near the fair. Daylight streamed into his eyes. It was morning.

In front of him, the embers of what was once Dreamland still glowed.

As Ben watched, the roof caved in with a huge shower of sparks. Somehow, he had managed to get out right in the nick of time.

Nearby, Ben saw the flashing lights of fire engines. Firemen were aiming hoses, trying to stop the fire from spreading to the other tents. People were standing anxiously in groups, talking quietly.

Ben saw his parents walking quickly into the area. They walked up to him.

Dad looked angry. Mom just looked relieved. They must have come looking for him when they noticed that he wasn't in bed.

"How did you find me?" asked Ben.

"When we saw that your bed hadn't been slept in, we guessed you must have come here," said Mom. "I'm just glad you're safe."

Together they stood and watched the fire destroying Dreamland forever.

"We've got some good news for you," said Mom. "I just called the hospital. Gran's out of danger. She's going to be okay."

"And the vet called. Jip's coming home today," said Dad.

"But the best news is that your dad is getting his old job back. They called this morning," said Mom. She looked happy.

"Not just my old job," said Dad. "The firm is expanding. They've given me a better job, with more money."

He looked at Ben. "It seems like our luck has changed," Dad said. He smiled for the first time in days.

Ben looked down.

He was holding something tightly in his hand. It was a strip of burned parchment, torn from the bottom of a page. His name was written on it in faded red ink.

As he watched, it crumpled into ash. Then, gently, it blew away in the early morning light.

A group of people on their way to school came up to watch the end of the fire. Lisa was with them.

"You're safe," she said. "I'm so glad." She gave Ben a hug.

Ben heaved a huge sigh of relief.

nin
Be

Everything was going to be all right.

"Time to go home," said Mom.

They turned away. All that was left of Dreamland was a heap of smoking ash.

* * *

A few days later, it was the last night of the fair. Ben had gone with Lisa and some other friends for some last-minute fun.

At first, he hadn't wanted to go, but he was really enjoying himself. It was great. He could enjoy the fair, since now he had nothing to worry about.

Dreamland was gone for good. It had burned to the ground. Ben was safe.

They went on all the rides, laughing and shouting. They ate cotton candy and won stuffed animals.

Just as they were leaving, Ben spotted something that made him rub his eyes. He wandered toward it to get a clearer view.

Dreamland, said the lights of the sideshow. Ben saw the showman. He had his hand on a boy's shoulder. Ben realized it was Mark.

Mark was being led toward a little door at the side of the stage.

Ben was too far away to be sure, but he thought the man looked straight at him. His smile seemed to say, "No hard feelings." Mark smiled too as he went through the door.

Ben shuddered.

The showman laughed, showing his long, wolf-like teeth.

This time Ben got the message loud and clear.

"There are always people around who like a bargain," it said. "We sign them up at Dreamland every day."

DREAM
COME IN IF YOU DARE!

ABOUT THE AUTHOR

Phil Preece was an English teacher for twenty-five years before he decided to become a writer. He also writes theater reviews and writes and directs plays.

ABOUT THE ILLUSTRATOR

Bradford Kendall has enjoyed drawing for as long as he can remember. As a boy, he loved to read comic books and watch old monster movies. He graduated from the Rhode Island School of Design with a BFA in Illustration. Bradford lives in Providence, Rhode Island.

GLOSSARY

attempt (uh-TEMPT)—try to do something

bargain (BAR-guhn)—an agreement

contract (KON-trakt)—a signed agreement

dare (DAIR)—if you dare to do something, you are brave enough to do it

expressions (ek-SPRESH-uhnz)—the looks on peoples' faces

parchment (PARCH-muhnt)—heavy paper

prey (PRAY)—something that is being hunted

pursuers (pur-SOO-urz)—the people who are following or chasing someone

showman (SHOH-man)—the person who presents a show

triumphant (trye-UHMF-ant)—successful

DISCUSSION QUESTIONS

1. What was the agreement that Ben made with the showman? Why did he make it?

2. When Ben goes back to the fair, Dreamland looks completely different. Why do you think that was? Talk about it.

3. If you were at Dreamland, would you sign the contract? Why or why not?

WRITING PROMPTS

1. What's your favorite thing to do at a fair or carnival? Write about it.

2. Ben has some bad things happen to him and his family in this book. He also has some good things happen. Make up another set of good and bad things that happen to Ben.

3. This book is a scary story. Write your own scary story!

MORE SHADE BOOKS!

Take a deep breath and

On her birthday, Rebecca Chantry receives a present she doesn't want—an old piece of embroidery with her name sewn on it. Then someone else stares back when she looks in the mirror. Who is the other Rebecca Chantry? What will it take to stop her?

step into the shade!

On Simon Prints's fourteenth-and-a-half birthday, he wakes up in the middle of the night with a tail. The transformation has begun. A few days later, Simon has hair covering his body. In a matter of weeks, he's become a wolfanoid: half-boy, half-beast.